The WIZARD of Oz™
Movie Storybook

Mia & Noa Alonso

WB WORLDWIDE PUBLISHING™

SCHOLASTIC INC.

New York Toronto London Auckland Sydney
Mexico City New Delhi Hong Kong

ISBN 0-590-63268-X

Published by Scholastic Inc.

12 11 10 9 8 7 6 5   2 3/0

Cover and interior designed by Joan Ferrigno

Printed in the U.S.A.

First Scholastic printing, December 1998

Dorothy and her little dog Toto hurried down a dusty Kansas road to the family farm.

"Aunt Em!" Dorothy called, flinging open the gate. "Listen to what Miss Gulch did to Toto. She —"

"Dorothy, please!" Aunt Em interrupted. "We're trying to count the baby chicks."

"Don't bother us now, honey," Uncle Henry added gently.

Her aunt and uncle were working too hard to listen, but Dorothy felt so upset, she couldn't stop. "Miss Gulch hit Toto with a rake," she continued, "just because he gets in her garden and chases her cat!"

"Dorothy! We're busy!" Aunt Em said, once and for all.

Maybe the farmhands will listen, Dorothy thought. She hurried to the farmyard, where Hunk, Hickory, and Zeke were fixing a wagon.

"Now lookit, Dorothy," Hunk told her. "You have to use your head about Miss Gulch. Think you didn't have any brains at all."

Hickory stepped stiffly into the barn. "It feels like I'm all rusted," Hickory complained. Then he turned to Dorothy. "Miss Gulch is just an old sour face. She ain't got no heart."

Zeke, herding pigs into the pen, said, "Miss Gulch ain't nothing to be afraid of. Have a little courage, that's all."

Nobody really listened to her. Nobody understood. "Do you suppose there's a place without any troubles?" Dorothy asked Toto. "There must be, far far away. Behind the moon. Beyond the rain. Somewhere, over the rainbow."

For a moment Dorothy was lost in a dream, imagining bluebirds, blue skies, and colorful rainbows.

But then she heard the creak of a bicycle and a cackling laugh. It was Miss Gulch — with a sheriff's order to take Toto away!

"That dog's a menace!" Miss Gulch exclaimed to Aunt Em and Uncle Henry. "And he's going to be destroyed."

"You wicked old witch!" Dorothy cried. "Uncle Henry! Auntie Em! Don't let her take him!"

But Miss Gulch showed them the order, and they couldn't go against the law. Uncle Henry put Toto in Miss Gulch's bicycle basket, and off she rode. Sobbing, Dorothy turned away. But a little way down the road, Toto poked his head out of the basket. He quickly jumped out and scampered back to Dorothy.

"Toto, darling!" Dorothy cried, hugging her dog tight. "They'll be coming for you any minute. We've got to run away!"

Swiftly, Dorothy packed a suitcase, tucked Toto under her arm, and headed down the road. Soon, she crossed a bridge and came to a campsite. A wagon stood nearby with the words "PROFESSOR MARVEL" printed in big letters on the side.

That must be the Professor, Dorothy thought, spying a kindly white-haired man sitting by the fire.

Professor Marvel traveled the country telling fortunes, and he guessed — practically right away — that Dorothy was running away from home.

He led Dorothy inside the wagon to look into his crystal ball. Dorothy closed her eyes and the Professor peeked into her suitcase, spying a photo.

"I see a house with a picket fence," he exclaimed, "and a woman, wearing a polka-dot dress."

"Aunt Em!" cried Dorothy.

"She's crying," the Professor went on. "Someone has just about broken her heart."

Dorothy jumped up. She had to see Aunt Em! "Come on, Toto," she called, and they raced back up the road, hurrying to get home.

The wind was gusting strongly now. Dorothy struggled across the bridge. The skies grew dark. A storm was brewing — a twister!

At the farm, Uncle Henry locked everything up tight. "Dorothy!" Aunt Em shouted into the wind. "Where are you?"

Aunt Em kept calling, but the storm raged too fiercely for her voice to carry. They had to take shelter now, so they shut the cellar door behind them. A minute later, Dorothy stumbled into the house.

Where is everyone? wondered Dorothy. Frightened by the storm, scared of being alone, she sat on the edge of her bed, holding Toto tight.

Suddenly a window blew loose. It flew through the air, hitting Dorothy on the head. For a moment, everything went black. Then Dorothy saw a swirling column of dust. It was lifting the house off the ground!

Spinning . . . spinning . . . they were whirling inside the twister . . . until finally, they crashed back down.

Curious and a little frightened, Dorothy edged to the front door. Then she stepped outside, gazing in wonder. Flowers, trees, grass . . . they were all brighter and more colorful than she'd ever seen.

"Toto," Dorothy whispered. "I've a feeling we're not in Kansas anymore. We must be over the rainbow!"

A glimmering bubble floated close to Dorothy, and suddenly beautiful Glinda, Good Witch of the North, stood in its place.

"Are you a good witch or a bad witch?" Glinda asked.

"Who me?" Dorothy stammered. "I'm not a witch at all. I'm Dorothy Gale, from Kansas."

"You are in Munchkinland now," Glinda explained.

Munchkinland was a part of Oz, where shy little people called Munchkins lived.

"The Munchkins called me," Glinda continued, "because a new witch dropped a house on the Wicked Witch of the East."

Dorothy gazed at the house and stepped back. A pair of feet stuck out from the bottom, wearing black-and-white stockings and glittering ruby slippers.

"Tee-hee, tee-hee." Dorothy heard soft giggles. Joyful voices. She gazed all around, but she didn't see a soul. Then, one by one, pint-sized smiling people stepped out from behind flowers and trees. The Munchkins!

"The Munchkins are happy because you have freed them from the Wicked Witch of the East," Glinda explained.

"Ding dong, the Witch is dead," the Munchkins sang gleefully. One by one, they gathered around to thank Dorothy.

All at once a tremendous boom echoed through Munchkinland. A cloud of red smoke filled the air, and the Munchkins scattered in fear as another witch — the Wicked Witch of the West — suddenly appeared.

"Who killed my sister?" the Witch cried hoarsely. She whirled to face Dorothy. "Was it you?"

"It was an accident!" Dorothy told her quickly. "I didn't mean to kill anybody!"

"Well, my little pretty," the Witch laughed. "I can cause accidents too."

She raised her broomstick in anger, but then she remembered the ruby slippers. Turning from Dorothy, she reached for the glittering shoes. Suddenly, the stockings shriveled up and the slippers disappeared under the house — only to reappear on Dorothy's feet!

The witch hissed, "What have you done with the ruby slippers? Give them back to me or I'll . . . "

But Glinda stopped her. She pointed to Dorothy's feet. "It's too late! There they are and there they'll stay."

"Their magic must be very powerful," Glinda whispered to Dorothy. "Or she wouldn't want them so badly! Be gone!" she called to the Witch. "Before somebody drops a house on you too!"

The Witch cackled. "Very well. But just try to stay out of my way," she threatened Dorothy. "I'll get you, my pretty, and your little dog too!"

A clap of thunder echoed over the land, and the Wicked Witch disappeared in a burst of fire and smoke.

Witches! Warnings! More than anything in the world, Dorothy wanted to go home. "Which is the way to Kansas?" she asked. "How can I get home?"

"The only person who might know is the great and wonderful Wizard of Oz," Glinda explained.

The Wizard lived in the Emerald City, a long journey from Munchkinland. But how would Dorothy get there?

"All you do is follow the Yellow Brick Road," Glinda said.

"Follow the Yellow Brick Road," the Munchkins echoed, leading Dorothy to its very beginning. "Follow the Yellow Brick Road!"

Soon Dorothy came to a crossroads. She paused. "*Now* which way do we go?" she asked Toto, confused.

"*That* way is a very nice way," said a voice behind her.

Dorothy whirled around. There was nobody there, only a scarecrow in a cornfield, one arm pointing down the road. Toto barked at the stuffed man of straw.

"Don't be silly, Toto," Dorothy said. "Scarecrows don't talk!"

But then the Scarecrow spoke again. "It's pleasant *that* way too," and he pointed in the other direction.

Dorothy was beginning to believe anything was possible in Oz. So she helped the Scarecrow down from his pole. Then she watched in amazement as a band of crows settled on his shoulder.

"I can't even a scare a crow," moaned the Scarecrow. "Oh, I'm a failure. And all because I haven't got a brain."

"I'm going to the Emerald City to see the Wizard," Dorothy told the Scarecrow. "So he can help me get back home."

"Maybe he could give me some brains!" exclaimed the Scarecrow. "Won't you take me with you?"

"Of course I will!" agreed Dorothy. "Hooray! We're off to see the Wizard!"

The two skipped merrily down the road, until they came to a grove of apple trees. Feeling hungry, Dorothy picked a bright red apple.

"What do you think you're doing?" the tree shouted, grabbing it back.

"Oh dear," Dorothy said, surprised. "I keep forgetting I'm not in Kansas."

But the Scarecrow knew how to get some apples for her: by pretending they had worms.

The trees grew so angry, they flung the apples right to Dorothy and the Scarecrow.

One apple rolled deeper into the woods. Dorothy chased it. She almost bumped into a man of tin, rusted stiff.

"Oil can," the Tin Man croaked out of the corner of his mouth. "Oil can."

Dorothy found the can nearby and quickly oiled the Tin Man so he could move.

"I was chopping that tree," the Tin Man explained, tilting from side to side, "when suddenly it started to rain, and I rusted solid."

"Well, you're perfect now," said Dorothy.

"Perfect?" the Tin Man said sadly. A tear trickled down his cheek. "Bang on my chest. It's empty. The tinsmith forgot to give me a heart."

"Come with us," declared Dorothy. "You can ask the Wizard of Oz for one!"

Before the Tin Man could say a word, cackling laughter rang through the woods. The Wicked Witch landed with her broomstick on the roof of the Tin Man's house.

"Helping the little lady along, are you, my fine gentlemen?" she cried. "Well, stay away from her!"

Still laughing, she jumped on her broomstick and flew away. But her threats did no good. The Scarecrow and the Tin Man were more determined than ever to go to Emerald City with Dorothy.

The woods grew thicker now, the sun barely peeking through the trees. "I don't like this forest," Dorothy whispered, scared. "It's dark and creepy. Do you suppose we'll meet any wild animals?

"Lions?" she asked softly. "And tigers?" said the Scarecrow. The Tin Man nodded. "And bears!"

Lions and tigers and bears? "Oh my!" said Dorothy as they followed the twisting road.

All of a sudden, a lion leaped onto the road. "Grrr!" he roared. "Put 'em up! Which one of you first? I'll fight you all!" Everyone backed away from the ferocious creature, except Toto, who barked loudly.

"I'll get you, peewee!" the Lion shouted.

"Shame on you!" cried Dorothy, stepping forward to swat the Lion on the nose. "Picking on a poor little dog."

"Well, you didn't have to go and hit me," the Lion sobbed fearfully. "Is my nose bleeding?"

"Of course not," Dorothy told him. "Why, you're nothing but a great big coward!"

"You're right," the Lion admitted, hanging his head. "I *am* a coward. I even scare myself."

"I'm sure the Wizard can give you some courage," Dorothy told him. "He's going to give the Tin Man a heart and the Scarecrow some brains."

"And take Dorothy home," the Scarecrow added.

So the Lion linked arms with the others, and they all set off down the Yellow Brick Road.

Dorothy smiled at her new friends. It was funny, but she felt as if she had known them all the time.

Not far away, the Wicked Witch watched Dorothy in her crystal ball. "I'll take care of you now," she cried. "And when I get those slippers, my powers will be greatest in Oz." She rubbed her hands together, plotting exactly what to do.

"Something with poison in it," she mused. "But attractive to the eye. Poppies!"

Dorothy and her friends left the forest and came to a beautiful field of poppy flowers. Towers gleamed in the distance.

"Emerald City!" shouted Dorothy. "We're almost there!"

The friends skipped through the pretty poppies. "Come on, come on," urged the Scarecrow.

But Dorothy couldn't keep up with the others. Tired, she put her hand to her head and said slowly, "I can't run anymore. I have to rest."

The Lion yawned. "Come to think of it, forty winks wouldn't be bad."

Dorothy, the Lion, and Toto lay down among the poppies and closed their eyes. There was no waking them at all. The Scarecrow was . . . scared!

Why, it's the Wicked Witch, it must be *her* doing, he suddenly realized — the Witch cast a spell on the poppies to make Dorothy sleepy!

"Help!" called the Scarecrow. "Help!" called the Tin Man.

Far away, Glinda heard their cries. She waved her wand and snow began to fall over the field.

"Oh!" shouted the Scarecrow. "Maybe that will help."

Dorothy opened her eyes.

The Lion stretched. "Unusual weather we're having, ain't it?" he asked, surprised at the snowfall.

The Scarecrow was right; the snow *did* help! Jumping up, Dorothy and the others linked arms once more. "Let's go!" said Dorothy. "Emerald City is closer and prettier than ever!"

Once inside Emerald City, Dorothy gazed around in wonder. People bustled all about, sidewalks sparkled, and a horse of a different color drove them down the street — a horse that changed from brown to blue to all the colors of a rainbow.

Dorothy and her friends laughed, eager to see the Wizard. They didn't know that at that very moment, the Wicked Witch was jumping on her broomstick, flying from her castle — right in their direction.

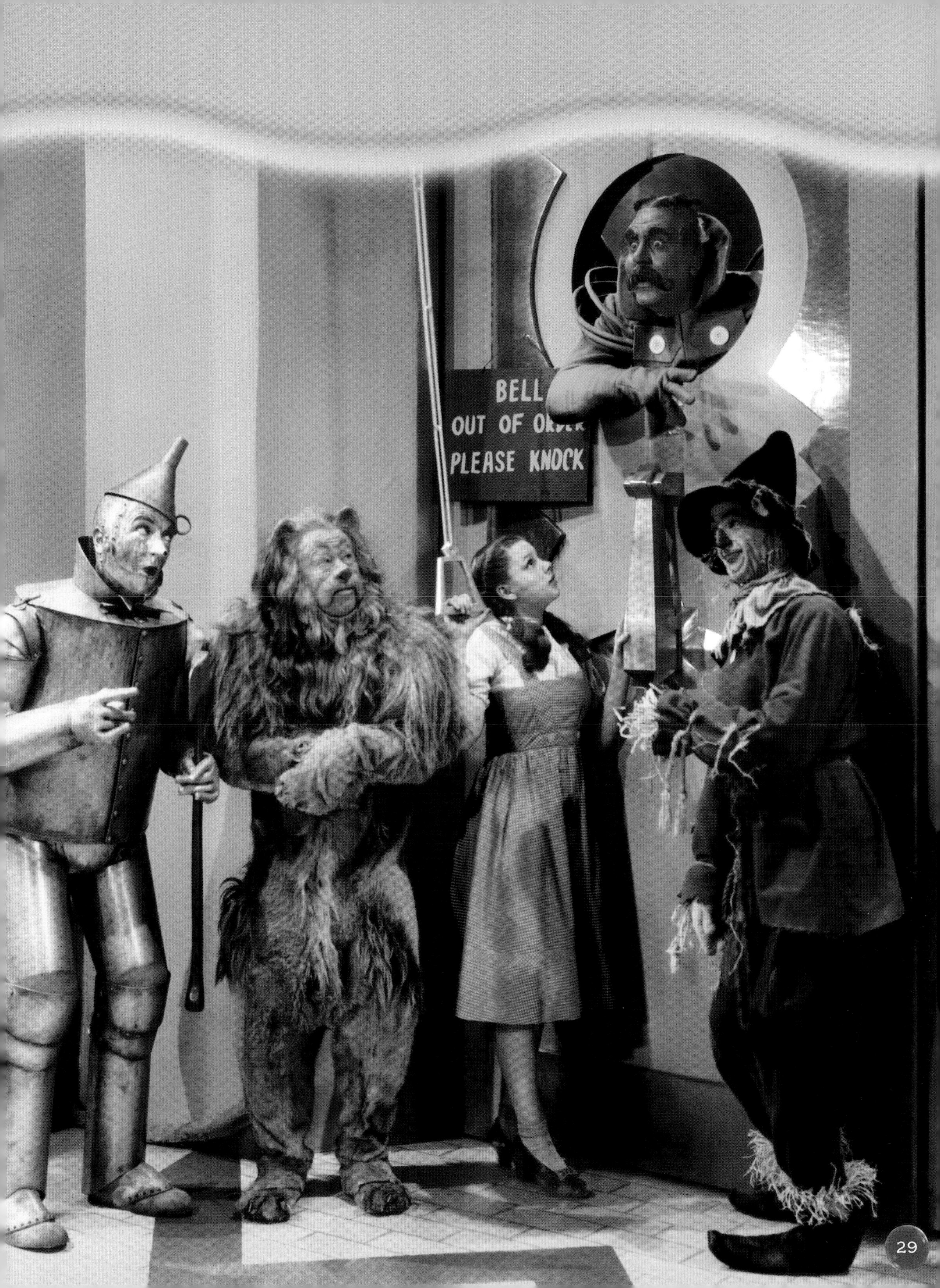
BELL
OUT OF ORDER
PLEASE KNOCK

But suddenly, people gasped and pointed at a dark figure riding a broom in the sky. Black smoke curled behind the broom, etching the words SURRENDER DOROTHY in the bright blue sky.

"It's the Witch!" cried Dorothy. "She followed us here!"

"Who's Dorothy?" one woman asked.

"The Wizard will explain it!" said another, and the crowd hurried to the palace.

"Everything is all right!" the palace guard assured them. "The great and powerful Oz has matters well in hand. You can all go home."

Relieved, the townspeople scattered. Only Dorothy and her friends remained.

"Orders are, nobody can see the Wizard," the guard told them. "Not nobody, not nohow."

"But *she's* Dorothy!" the Scarecrow explained, thinking quickly.

The guard's eyes opened wide. "I'll announce you at once!"

The gates swung open. The Lion hung back, afraid. But the others took his hand and helped him down the long dark corridor into a vast room with a giant throne in the middle. Flames and smoke billowed from a glittering chair, and the outline of a man's head wavered amidst it all.

"I am Oz," a deep voice intoned. "The great and powerful!"

Dorothy trembled. But she had to step forward, had to ask for the Tin Man's heart, the Lion's courage, and the Scarecrow's brain.

"If you please," stammered Dorothy. "I am Dorothy, the small and meek. We've come to ask you —"

"Silence!" thundered the voice. "Oz knows why you have come, and has every intention of granting your requests. But first you must prove yourselves worthy. You must perform a very small task. Bring me the broomstick of the Wicked Witch of the West!" he boomed.

The Lion gasped. The Witch's broomstick? Why, she'd never give it up. Still, they *had* to try. But first, they had to find the Wicked Witch's castle.

They entered the Haunted Forest and came across a sign: WITCHES CASTLE 1 MILE. I'D TURN BACK IF I WERE YOU!

The Lion whirled around, ready to do just that. But the Scarecrow and the Tin Man grasped him firmly, determined to go on.

Watching from her crystal ball, the Witch laughed. Then she turned to Nikko, leader of her army of Winged Monkeys. "Now bring me that girl and her dog!" she ordered. "I want those ruby slippers!"

The Winged Monkeys flew over the forest, until they spotted Dorothy and Toto below. They swooped down. Two monkeys lifted Dorothy by the arms, and another scooped up Toto — all before the Scarecrow, the Lion, or the Tin Man could stop them.

"What a nice little dog!" the Wicked Witch exclaimed when the monkeys brought them into her tower room moments later. Sneering nastily, she grabbed Toto onto her lap.

"Give him back!" Dorothy demanded.

"All in good time, my pretty," cackled the Witch. "When you give me those slippers!"

Dorothy shook her head. Glinda had told her not to give them up — no matter what.

"Very well!" cried the Witch. She put Toto in a basket. "Toss him in the river and drown him!"

"No!" said Dorothy quickly. "You can have your old slippers!"

The Witch snickered with joy, eagerly reaching for them. She curled her fingers over the shoes . . . she almost had them . . . but suddenly sparks flew from Dorothy's feet!

"Ah!" cried the Witch, jumping back in pain. "I should have known. Those slippers will never come off, as long as you're alive!"

Just then Toto poked his head out of the basket and dashed out the door.

"Run, Toto, run!" Dorothy shouted as the monkeys gave chase. Castle guards tossed their spears, but Toto raced over the drawbridge and into the forest.

Angered, the Witch turned over a huge hourglass. "That's how much longer you've got to be alive!" she shrieked, locking Dorothy in the tower room.

Toto found the Scarecrow, the Lion, and the Tin Man deep in the forest. He barked once, then twice more. The Scarecrow understood. He told the others, "Why, don't you see? He's come to take us to Dorothy!"

Quickly the Tin Man, the Lion, and the Scarecrow followed Toto over a rocky hillside to the Witch's castle. Disguising themselves in guard uniforms, they sneaked inside.

Still a prisoner in the tower, Dorothy gazed at the hourglass. Time was running out. Tears ran down her cheeks as she sobbed in fright.

"Dorothy!" called a voice. "Dorothy! Where are you?" Dorothy turned to the crystal ball. Inside she could see Auntie Em calling for her, worried.

"Oh, Auntie Em!" she cried. "I'm here in Oz. I'm trying to get home!"

But Aunt Em's face faded away, and suddenly the Witch loomed in the crystal, laughing wildly.

Just then, the Scarecrow and the others raced to the door. "Dorothy, it's us!" shouted the Lion.

The Tin Man lifted his ax and splintered the thick wood. Dorothy was free! She rushed out of the room. "Hurry!" said the Scarecrow quickly. "We've got no time to lose!"

The four friends rushed this way and that as guards gave chase down long corridors and up winding staircases. Which was the way out? How could they escape?

Suddenly guards were everywhere, surrounding Dorothy and the others. "Well," snarled the Witch, glaring at Dorothy. "The last to go will see the first three go before her!"

She thrust her broom up to a torch on the wall. "How about a little fire, Scarecrow?" she asked, jabbing the flaming broom at his straw.

"Help!" he shouted. "I'm burning!"

Quickly Dorothy tossed a nearby bucket of water over the Scarecrow, dousing the flames. Water splashed the Witch in the face.

"Oh!" screamed the Witch. "Look what you've done! I'm melting! I'm melting!"

She was melting . . . melting . . . the water making her disappear before their very eyes . . . until nothing was left but her cloak, hat, and broom.

"Hail to Dorothy!" cried the guards, happy to finally be free. "The Wicked Witch is dead!" They gave Dorothy the broom, and the four friends set off to see the Wizard again.

"Please sir," said Dorothy at the Wizard's palace. "We've done what you told us." She placed the broomstick by the throne. "So we'd like you to keep your promise."

"Go away!" the voice boomed louder than ever. "Come back tomorrow."

"Tomorrow?" cried Dorothy. "But I want to go home now!"

The Wizard shouted angrily as Toto wandered away to sniff a nearby curtain. Then the little dog tugged back the drapes. A man . . . a plain, ordinary man . . . was talking into a microphone, saying, "The great Oz has spoken!"

Hurriedly the man tried to pull the curtain back, but it was too late.

"Pay no attention to that man behind the curtain!" the voice yelled.

"Who are you?" asked Dorothy, puzzled.

"Well, I-I am the Wizard of Oz," the man stuttered. "There's no other Wizard except me."

"You're a very bad man," scolded Dorothy.

"Oh no, my dear," the Wizard said sadly. "I'm a very good man. Just a very bad Wizard."

"But what about the promises?" asked the Scarecrow.

Maybe he *could* do something about granting wishes.

The Wizard reached into a black bag. "Back where I come from," he told the Scarecrow, "we have universities, where men go to become great thinkers. They have no more brains than you have. But they do have a diploma!" Then he handed the Scarecrow an honorary degree. It was a ThD, doctor of thinkology.

The Scarecrow grinned, placed his finger to his head — and recited mathematical formulas!

Then the Wizard gave the Lion a medal of valor for all his bravery against Wicked Witches. He gave the Tin Man a ticking watch in the shape of a heart as a testimonial of esteem and affection.

Then the Wizard turned to Dorothy. "I'm an old Kansas man myself," he explained. "While performing with my balloon at a carnival one day, I found myself floating away . . . finally landing here! And now, Dorothy, you and I will return!"

In no time at all, the balloon was set up in Emerald Square. The Wizard, Dorothy, and Toto climbed into the basket, and all the townspeople gathered to see them off.

But at that moment, Toto spied a cat. He jumped out of Dorothy's arms to chase it, disappearing into the crowd.

"Toto!" cried Dorothy. She climbed out after him, just as the balloon began to rise.

"Don't go without me!" Dorothy pleaded to the Wizard. She found Toto on the edge of the crowd and hurried back to the platform. "Come back!"

"I can't!" called the Wizard, floating high in the sky. "I don't know how it works!"

He waved to the people below, and then he was gone.

"Oh," Dorothy cried, "now I'll never get home."

"Stay with us, Dorothy," the Lion told her tearfully. "We all love you."

Dorothy loved them too, and it was hard saying good-bye. But she belonged somewhere else. Home.

Suddenly a shimmering bubble appeared. It was Glinda! "You've always had the power to go back to Kansas," the Good Witch kindly explained. "But you had to learn it for yourself."

Dorothy thought a moment. "Why," she exclaimed, surprised, "it wasn't enough just to want to see Uncle Henry and Auntie Em. If I ever go looking for my heart's desire again, I won't look any further than my own backyard. Because if it isn't there, I never really lost it to begin with!"

Finally Dorothy realized she didn't have to run away at all!

Dorothy turned to her friends one last time. "Now I know I've got a heart," the Tin Man told her. "Because it's breaking."

"Good-bye, Tin Man," Dorothy said softly. Then she turned to the Lion. "You know," she told him, "I'm going to miss the way you hollered for help before you found your courage."

"I would never have found it if wasn't for you," the Lion said, trying to be strong.

Then Dorothy hugged the Scarecrow tight. "I think I'll miss you most of all," she whispered. "I'm ready now."

"Now," said Glinda, "close your eyes and tap your heels together three times."

Dorothy held Toto tight, clicked her heels, and repeated after Glinda: "There's no place like home. There's no place like home."

Dorothy opened her eyes and saw the farmhands bent over her bed, watching her worriedly. Aunt Em, Uncle Henry, and Professor Marvel were there too. Finally she was home!

"Lie quiet," Aunt Em said. "You've had a bump on your head and you've been dreaming."

"No," said Dorothy, "I went away where some of it wasn't nice, but most of it was beautiful." She gazed at Hunk, Hickory, Zeke, and Professor Marvel. "And you, and you, and you were there!"

She hugged Toto close. "Oh, but anyway, Toto! We're home! And you're all here. And I'm not going to leave here ever, ever again because I love you all. And oh, Auntie Em, there's no place like home."